POPPER'S

MICHAEL KINGSWOOD

New customers come through Popper's bookstore all the time. But one of them, an average man in every way, has David very concerned that he intends more than just buying books.

Popper's is a 4,100 word short mystery.

Enjoy the book! After you're done, please come to Michael's website and sign up for his mailing list at michaelkingswood.com/newsletter-signup/. Guaranteed to be spam free, he uses it to announce new releases and special promotions for his fans.

Popper's

It was nearing the end of David's shift at Popper's Books And Things. Even for a Tuesday, it had been a slow day. Maybe half a dozen people had actually bought something all day; not for the first time, he pondered whether working the counter at a small bookstore was the best summer job for him to have taken.

He was an Engineering major, not in the liberal arts. He probably should have pushed to find something more related to his field.

But he couldn't even apply for a summer intern position until after the end of next school year, and there was something about Popper's…

He'd discovered it his second week at school, and before long it had become the place he hung out in more than any other.

The antique but carefully preserved and polished mahogany counter running half the length of the store to the right of the entrance, where the staff kept watch over the customers like a bartender looking out over his pub.

The six rows of equally-polished hardwood shelves—not mahogany but still nice—that took up the center of the shop's space.

The wall shelves to the left of the entrance that housed new release comics of every variety, and the backlist boxes at the rear.

The small brown leather couch against the wall past the end of the counter, and the two matching stuffed chairs opposite it where customers could read or sip a cup from the pot that Barbara, the owner, insisted be maintained freshly-brewed and available at all times.

And, of course, the game room in back, complete with all the miniatures a game master and his groups of players could need for the evening, an old and battered but still running refrigerator where the players could stash snacks and—non-alcoholic—drinks, and a trio of tables sized for eight so that there was almost always room to get a game on.

Barbara kept the shelves well-stocked with a mix of new and used tomes, and liked to spray the place down with a different air freshener each week. Today, that meant the place had the mixed odor of french roast and lavender, with just a hint of old paper beneath.

Add the light jazz that made up the shop's approved playlist, piped from the cashier's iMac to bluetooth speakers nestled at each corner of the shop's main room, and it was a nice, homey, welcoming place.

Just lacking in customers. Today, at least.

David had the register app open on the iMac and was just getting started reconciling the take for his shift—not a hard task today—when the little bell mounted above the entrance rang.

A customer.

He looked up, and his hackles rose immediately.

The guy was average looking. As average as it

was possible to be: height, build, facial features, hair…all the way down to his beige suit. He would have had to work to be more unnoticeable.

Except that as he approached David's counter, doffing the sunglasses he had been wearing to reveal light brown eyes, he gave off a sense of presence, of power right on the edge of control, and David knew this was no ordinary, average guy, however he may look.

"Can I help you?"

The guy folded up his shades and slipped them into the inner pocket of his suit coat. He remained silent for a couple seconds, and glanced to his left, toward the gaming room. Checking to see if anyone was back there?

Finally, the man looked back at David, and the intensity of that very average stare made him want to shift on his feet.

"I don't know, David. Can you help me?"

David swallowed. "How do you know my name?"

The man's lips turned upward into the smallest hint of a smile. "Store's website," he said, and David felt heat rise to his cheeks in embarrassment.

He'd forgotten about the staff pictures Barbara posted there; it had seemed silly to put him up since he was just around for the summer, but she'd insisted.

The man let a few seconds pass in silence, then made a little shrug and looked toward the back room again. "Is Barbara here?"

"No, she's coming in for the evening shift today. Should be here in twenty minutes or so."

"Ah." He nodded as though David had said something profound.

"There's coffee if you want to wait for her."

"No, I must be off. Just tell her Henry said

hello, and I look forward to catching up with her soon."

Then he turned and walked out. David couldn't help thinking the plain name suited his plainness perfectly.

It made him distinctly uneasy.

By the time Barbara showed up—thirty minutes later—he still had not been able to put the guy out of his mind. Something was just…off…about him, and the whole situation there.

Barbara was all smiles, as usual, as she walked in the door. She had her reddish-brown hair up, her curls mostly bundled away in an intricate mass of braids and twists and what-have-yous that was impossible to follow, and wore jeans and a loose green collared blouse. In her mid 30s, she was a bit on the plump side, but what she lacked in sexiness she made up for in good old fashioned fun personality.

"Hey David," she said, as she swept through the door and over to the counter. "Good day?"

He shrugged. "Slow day."

"Well, it's Tuesday," she said, and maneuvered down toward the coffee pot over next to the couch.

"Yeah." David logged out of the register app and picked up his backpack, from where he had left it in the corner behind the counter. "Accounts are all square."

Barbara nodded, not taking her eyes away from the cup she was pouring. "Ok, thanks. Have a great night."

"You too." David slipped out from behind the counter, maneuvering carefully to avoid bumping into her as he passed her by. "By the way," he said as he started toward the door, "your friend Henry stopped by to say hi."

"What?"

The sudden change in her tone made him turn back to look at her, concern rising within him. She sounded like she really hoped she had heard him wrong.

"Henry. Plain guy. Really average, but…also not? He said hi, and that he wants to see you again soon."

Her hand that was holding the cup began to shake, and then the coffee she was pouring into the cup ran over.

Barbara made a yelp of pain and chagrin as the scalding liquid spilled over onto her hand. She reflexively shook the hand, flinging the coffee off, but lost her grip on the cup.

It fell and shattered on the false-wood laminate floor, coffee spilling all over the place.

"Damn!" Barbara said, and raised her burned hand to her mouth.

"Are you ok?" David said, rushing toward her.

She put the pot back down and waved him away. "I'm fine. I'm fine. Just…you surprised me."

"Let me help clean up."

"No. No, you go. You're seeing Lindsay again tonight right?" She put on a smile, but David could tell it was forced. "Don't want to be late."

No. No, he really didn't. Lindsay was something else. But… "You sure you're alright?" He glanced toward the door, recalling the look on Henry's face when he'd been there earlier. "Who is that guy?"

"Just…a friend. An old friend."

"Boyfriend?" He tried to make his tone light, but failed and he knew it.

Barbara shrugged. "The one that got away. Kind of?" Again with the smile that really wasn't. "Go on, get out of here."

David hesitated, and she made a shooing gesture. "Go!"

He went.

———

DAVID HAD the evening shift Thursday. When he came into the Popper's, Henry was there, with Barbara.

Henry had on the same beige suit as before, and stood in front of the counter in the same casual, yet also not, pose that he had used before.

Barbara was behind the counter, in her red and white stripped shirt and wearing a not happy expression.

When the bell over the door rang, announcing David's presence, both of them turned to look his way.

Barbara immediately tried—and failed—to put a relaxed smile on her face.

Henry gave David a once-over, then sniffed ever so softly. He looked back at Barbara and said, "Three days. Think about it."

Then he turned away from the counter and walked out. "David," Henry said as he walked past. It was both greeting and dismissal. And then he was gone.

David watched the door close behind him, then looked back at Barbara, both eyebrows raising.

Barbara met his gaze for a second, then looked away toward the iMac screen. "It's been a busy day," she said, and began typing away at the keyboard. "But I've got the accounts register up to date. There are two groups in the back."

David nodded, though she couldn't see, and moved over to the counter. "What was going on there?"

Barbara's lips compressed. She continued typing, but didn't reply.

"Barbara - "

"It's not your concern," she snapped, and David flinched.

She had never raised her voice like that, to anyone. Not in most of the year that he had been coming here, and that he had known her.

Barbara seemed to realize she had crossed a line. She stopped typing and just looked at the screen for a few seconds. Then, with a sigh, she turned her eyes back onto David.

"I appreciate you're worried, but you don't need to be. It's just some old business Henry and I have to resolve. I'm a big girl; I can handle it." She grinned mischievously then, and added, "And you have better things to be thinking about. You never told me how it went with Lindsay the other night."

It was a painfully obvious change in subject. She didn't want him involved with whatever was going on between her and David, that much was clear.

And, he reminded himself, she was almost twice his age. Pretty sure she knew how to handle herself.

So he went with the change in subject.

This time.

HENRY DIDN'T COME AROUND AGAIN that David saw, but the effects of his presence lingered. Barbara seemed distracted, and on-edge, as the work-week ended and the weekend began.

Normally David would not work the weekend. Barbara had a couple part-timers who handled the counter on Saturdays and Sundays, and though

Popper's was open late on Saturday she closed up early on Sundays, so there really wasn't any need for him.

But he found himself in the shop more often than not most weekends anyway. His D&D group met there Saturday afternoons, and a lot of the time there was a writer on a signing tour or something else cool going on so he ended up sticking around after the game.

This weekend, he decided he was going to keep as close an eye on the shop—and Barbara—as he could. Henry had said something was going down in three days. That meant Sunday. And though Barbara's assurance that there wasn't a problem stymied David's initial suspicions, her continued obvious discomfort made him determined to help.

If he could.

So he stayed late after his D&D game, until closing time. Lindsay wanted to hook up that night, but he begged off, honestly saying a friend needed his help.

Still, as he sat on the couch in Popper's and read the latest Grisham book while Henry steadfastly didn't come into the shop and Barbara had absolutely no difficulty at all all night, David wondered what the hell he thought he was doing.

SUNDAY DAWNED BRIGHT AND SUNNY, and David went out for his morning run.

While he was making his way through mile 3, he let his thoughts go, and he really considered what was going on. What he was doing.

Henry and Barbara had a previous relationship.

Something about Henry himself had certainly made David uncomfortable.

But maybe he was just projecting his own crap onto Barbara. She had seemed uncomfortable when he first mentioned Henry to her, but that was attributable to hearing from an old acquaintance after a long hiatus.

And David had no idea what he had stepped into when he arrived for work the other day. For all he knew, Henry had been trying to ask her out, and she felt embarrassed because David had walked in, not because of anything Henry had done.

She certainly didn't want to talk to David about it; but then she didn't really have to, did she? They were friendly, but she wasn't his friend. She was his boss, and quite a bit older than he was.

By the time he got home after his Sunday 5 miles, he convinced himself that he was just being silly.

And he had passed up a good, hot time with Lindsay last night, for nothing.

Dumbass.

He resolutely did not go to the shop. Instead, he met up with some friends for lunch.

He was just saying goodbye to them and heading for the bus stop to ride over to Lindsay's place when his cell phone rang. He looked at the screen. It was Popper's.

"Hello?"

"David, it's Sonya." Sonya was the part-timer who handled Sundays. "Have you heard from Barbara?"

He frowned and looked at the time. Almost three o'clock. "No, why?"

"Well, she usually comes by before closeup to check on things, but I haven't seen her. Did she tell you anything about it? I've never closed by myself. Should I just lock the door, or… ? But I don't have a key!"

"Have you tried calling her?"

"Yeah, it goes straight to voicemail."

David's frown grew, and a shiver went down his spine. This was completely unlike Barbara, and he immediately flashed to that brief interchange between her and Henry.

Three days. Think about it.

What had that guy done?

"David?"

He blinked, and came back to present. Sonya had been talking, but he had not heard a thing she'd said. Didn't matter, though.

"There's a spare key in the top drawer of the desk in the office behind the game room. Just shut down the computer, turn off the lights, and lock up. I've got the early shift tomorrow. You can bring the key back then."

"You sure? Ok, thanks."

She hung up.

David immediately tried calling Barbara himself.

Voicemail.

He swore under his breath. His mind raced, and he tried to think of what to do.

Call the cops?

And tell them what, that a grown woman hadn't returned a call? They'd tell him to take a hike.

He had Barbara's address with her contact information in his phone. He looked at it, uncertain.

Maybe she was just running late, and Sonya was being flighty. Or maybe she and Henry had hooked up, for real.

Or maybe he was doing something horrible to

her, that David would hear about tomorrow on the breaking news.

Screw it.

He opened up his Uber app.

DAVID HAD BEEN to Barbara's house once before, for an end-of-the-school-year party she'd thrown for her employees and friends of the store. It was a nicely maintained two bedroom bungalow on the north side of town, maybe a thousand square feet. Yellow siding with white trim, a porch the length of the house in front, a shingle roof, and a carport on a triangular lot that was stuck between two slightly-larger houses that were obviously by the same builder.

She had a stylized mailbox post that was carved in mermaids, and a mermaid-emblazoned welcome mat on her front porch. The lawn was closely trimmed, and she had chest-high screening bushes on either side of her lot. And that was it. No frills.

When David got out of the Uber, he saw that her car was in the driveway and her front door was slightly ajar. That wasn't necessarily an indication of trouble if she was home, but still, that anxious feeling that had been growing in his stomach since Sonya's call grew more intense.

He hurried up the walk from the street to the front door and stopped, listening.

A man's voice—he was sure it was Henry's—came through the crack between the door and the jamb. He sounded angry, but the voice was muffled so David couldn't make out what he was saying.

Adrenalin kicked in. Hard.

David slowly pushed the door open and fished his phone out.

The front sitting room was empty. David stepped inside and moved to the hallway that led back to the kitchen. There was a light on back there. Inching forward down the hall, he could hear Henry more clearly now.

" - not good enough, you dumb bitch."

Oh yeah. This wasn't good at all.

David called 911. The operator picked up, and he whispered, "There's an intruder in my friend's house." He gave the address.

The operator asked a question, but the sound of shattering glass from back in the kitchen overwhelmed David's hearing.

Before he could think about what he was doing, he surged forward and stepped into the kitchen.

Barbara was there, dressed in jeans and a white t-shirt. She was backed up against the wall opposite the doorway David had walked in through.

Henry was in front of her, his back to David. Again he had the beige suit on.

The glass David had heard breaking was lying at the base of the wall to Barbara's right, a jumbled pile of shards. Streaks of water flowed down the wall above the pile; Henry must have thrown the glass at the wall and it shattered there.

"There's nothing else, Henry," Barbara was saying as David stepped inside. "If you - " She saw him and her words cut off in a choking sound as her eyes went wide.

Henry noticed her change in demeanor. He made a quarter-turn to his left and looked behind himself. Seeing David there, his eyebrow rose.

"David. Nice to see you again." He no longer had the calm certitude he'd had the last couple times David had seen him, but the feeling of power was still there. It just was no longer in check. "Who you on the phone with?"

Only then did David realize he still had the phone up to his left ear, and that the 911 operator was talking.

"The cops," David said.

Henry made a tsking sound and shook his head. "Real sorry to hear that, kid."

He turned fully toward David and raised his right hand.

David saw the gun coming up to point at him, and everything seemed to slow to a crawl.

He wasn't old enough to get a carry permit yet, but his dad had spent a lot of time teaching him to shoot. One by one, his brain clicked past the rules of gun safety, as Henry violated them.

Treat every gun as if it's loaded. Ok, not really a violation, but…

Don't point the gun at anything you're not willing to shoot. Clear violation here.

Keep your finger off the trigger until you're ready to shoot.

Henry's trigger finger left its position along the slide of his pistol and slipped inside the trigger guard.

Oh crap, he *hadn't* violated rule number two, because he clearly was more than willing to shoot!

Duck!

The sound of a pistol shot turned time back to normal speed, but David didn't feel anything hit him, and Henry was close enough there was no way he could have missed.

Henry's arm dipped, and his expression became confused. He half-turned back toward Barbara, and a trickle of blood ran from the corner of his mouth.

"Barb- " he started to say.

She shot again. Henry's head jerked, and he collapsed to the floor.

David and Barbara stared at each other from across the room.

Her shirt was untucked on her right side, where she must have pulled it out to get at her concealed holster. The little pistol in her hands looked huge right then, and residual gunsmoke curled up from the end of its barrel.

She lowered the weapon to her side and said something, but David didn't actually hear it.

All he could hear was the pounding of his heart, the highly concerned babbling of the 911 operator, and, far away but getting closer by the second, the wailing of police sirens.

It took hours for the cops to get done with him. When he'd finally finished giving his statement and being interviewed, and interviewed, and re-interviewed, it was late and he wanted nothing but to go to bed.

He'd called his buddy Steve to come pick him up from the police station—an Uber didn't really seem like the thing right then—but Steve hadn't arrived yet, so he sat down on a bench in the public waiting section of the station.

He'd been sitting there for about five minutes when the door leading back into the innards of the station opened and Barbara walked out.

She looked just as beat as David felt, and she made a beeline toward the exit. But when she saw him, she stopped and walked over to the bench where he was sitting.

He watched her come, feeling numb and uncertain about everything. When she gestured toward the seat next to him, he just shrugged and she sat.

"I owe you an explanation," she said.

"That would be nice."

Barbara looked down a drew a breath. "When I was about your age, I got married. His name was Henry Popper." She looked back up into his eyes and raised an eyebrow.

David saw the import of the name immediately.

"He was everything you saw and more - dashing, exciting…and a criminal. I knew he was, but I didn't care. That was part of what made him so exciting and sexy. Well, he made this big heist, got a lot of money. And he got caught." Barbara shook her head. "After he went to prison I saw where my life would end up if I stuck with him. So I got a divorce."

"He went through all this because he was sore at you for dumping him?"

She shook her head. "The cops never found all the money he stole. But I knew where it was. I took it, changed my name, and moved away. I traveled for a while, and eventually ended up here. Used the money to buy a place and open my shop. Named it after him, for sentimental reasons I guess. Or maybe just stupidity. Regardless, after all this time I thought I'd covered my tracks, but…" She spread her hands.

"So he wanted his money back."

Barbara nodded. "With interest. But of course, the money was gone. Most of it. Into the house and the business. I thought…hoped…he'd accept a cut of the profits, let me pay him back over time. But…well, he was never as smart as he made on."

David nodded. It all made sense. But… "Are you going to be in trouble?"

Barbara looked askance at him. "No, of course not. It was a home invasion. I have a carry permit, but even if I didn't, he assaulted both of us with deadly force in my home. Totally justified shooting, morally and legally."

David had assumed that was the case from the beginning. "I meant about the money."

"Oh." She considered for a few seconds, then shrugged. "Statute of limitations for the heists he pulled are well past."

"Well, that's good I guess."

Barbara put her hand atop David's and gave his a little squeeze. "I'm sorry you had to go through that, David. More sorry than I can tell you."

"Yeah. Well, I - " David's phone buzzed, cutting him off.

He looked down and saw a text from Steve. He was out front.

David removed his hand from Barbara's and stood. "My ride's here. I gotta go."

Barbara's expression was unreadable. "Will I see you back at the shop, or - ?"

"I don't know. I need to think things through."

"I understand."

David nodded, then turned toward the exit. He stopped after half a dozen steps and turned back around to face her.

"Thanks for not letting him shoot me."

Barbara smiled, a sad little smile that said she feared their friendship was at an end. "You're welcome."

Then David walked out of the Police Station. He needed to rest, and think. And decide whether he would go back to the store that bore the name of the man Barbara had killed.

Or not.

Message From The Author

Thank you for reading my book. I hope you enjoyed reading it as much as I enjoyed writing it.

Every review helps an author out, so whether you loved this book, hated it, or something in between, please take a minute to tell other readers what you thought. All of the online retailers make it very easy to do, and I would really appreciate it.

Feel free to come say hi at my website or on Facebook. I always enjoy hearing from readers, especially since you all are, collectively, my boss.

I also have a weekly podcast, Story Time With Michael Kingswood, where I read stories and talk through some of the latest goings on in my world. I'd love to see you there.

Thanks again. My best to you and yours.

Warm Regards,
Michael Kingswood

Mailing List

If you enjoyed this book and would like word on new releases and special deals from Michael Kingswood, sign up for his newsletter on his website. Guaranteed to be spam-free, you can opt out at any time. And you can rest assured he will not share your information with anyone, for any reason.

https://michaelkingswood.com/newsletter-signup/

About The Author

Michael Kingswood is 20-year veteran of the US Navy submarine force and a lifelong fan of science fiction and fantasy literature. His work has appeared in numerous collections and anthologies, to include the Fiction River Anthology series from WMG publishing. He holds a bachelors degree in Mechanical Engineering as well as a Master of Engineering Management and a Master of Business Administration. He has four children and currently resides in San Diego.

Find Michael Kingswood online at:

www.michaelkingswood.com

www.facebook.com/michael.kingswood

steemit.com/@michaelkingswood

The Champion

Veritas Morte

Story Collections

Tales Of Adventure #1

Tales Of Adventure #2

Short Story 10-Pack

A Jar Of Mixed Treats

Short Mystery 10-Pack

Short Fiction

Michael has also published a number of shorter works,
links to which can be found on his website.